Other Kipper books

THE BLUE BALLOON
WHERE, OH WHERE, IS KIPPER'S BEAR?
KIPPER
KIPPER'S TOYBOX
KIPPER'S BIRTHDAY
KIPPER'S BOOK OF COLOUR
KIPPER'S BOOK OF WEATHER
KIPPER'S BOOK OF COUNTING
KIPPER'S BOOK OF OPPOSITES

First published 1996
by Hodder Children's Books,
a division of Hodder Headline plc,
338 Euston Road, London NW1 3BH

10 9 8 7 6 5 4 3 2 1

ISBN 0 340 65678 6

A catalogue record for this book
is available from the British Library.
The right of Mick Inkpen to be identified
as the author of this work
has been asserted by him.

Printed in Hong Kong

Kipper's Snowy Day

Mick Inkpen

Hodder
Children's
Books

A division of Hodder Headline plc

It was a new morning
and it was snowing!
Huge cotton wool snowflakes were
tumbling past Kipper's window.

'Yes!' said Kipper, jumping out
of his basket. 'Yes! Yes!'

He grabbed his scarf and wound
it three times round his head.
'Yes! Yes! Yes!'

Kipper was very positive
about snow.

Kipper rushed outside. The snow
lay deep and smooth and new, like an
empty page waiting to be scribbled on.
He made a paw print, and then another.

And then with a whoop he went charging round and round, crisscrossing this way and that, until the garden was full of his tracks.

Kipper stopped to catch his breath, letting the swirling snowflakes melt on his tongue. Then he fell backwards into the snow and lay there panting.

When he stood up he found that he had made a perfect Kipper shaped hole. He tried again. Then he tried a different shape. And another.

'I bet Tiger hasn't thought of this' he said, and ran off to find his best friend.

Kipper found Tiger at the top of Big Hill. He was wrapped up in a fat bundle of silly, woolly clothes. Kipper plopped a friendly snowball on top of his head.

'Hello,' said Tiger.

Tiger pointed up at the sky. A watery sun was seeping through the grey clouds.

'It won't last' he said. 'It'll all be gone by tomorrow. There's a warm wind coming'. Tiger was like that. He knew things.

But this was not at all what
Kipper wanted to hear, so he started
throwing snowballs at his friend.

Tiger was very easy to hit
because the silly, woolly clothes were
wrapped so tightly around him that
he could hardly move.
And his own snowballs
stuck like little pompoms
to the silly, woolly
gloves.

'Look at my new game,' said Kipper, falling backwards into the snow.

'You get up very carefully… and there you are!' And there he was, or at least the shape of him.

Tiger stretched out his arms, and fell backwards with a soft, woolly 'crump'. But when he tried to get up he could not. He was too round. He just lay there waving his arms and legs like a beetle on its back.

Tiger heaved himself over onto his tummy, but rolled too far, and found himself on his back again. He tried again. The same thing happened. Snow began to stick in thick lumps to the silly, woolly clothes. Crossly, he heaved himself over once more.

This time he rolled over twice, three times, four times...

Slowly at first,
and then a little faster,
and then a lot faster,
and then very fast indeed,
he rolled down the hill.

And as he went the silly, woolly
clothes picked up more and more
snow, so that by the time he
reached the bottom he had changed
from a small dog into a giant
snowball. The giant snowball
fell to pieces.

Kipper charged down the hill.

'Are you all right Tiger?' he panted.

Tiger pulled off his silly, woolly hat.

A big grin spread across his face.

'Again!' he said.

So that is what they did, all
day long, taking turns to wear the
silly, woolly clothes.

And by the time the sun began
to dip towards the hill, making their
shadows long and skinny, they had
rolled enough snow to the bottom to
build a giant snowdog.

They watched their shadows
lengthen and fade.

'It'll all be gone by tomorrow,'
said Tiger. 'There's a warm
wind coming.'

But for once
Tiger was wrong.
The warm wind stayed
away, and that night
another snowstorm smoothed out all
of Kipper's paw prints, making the
garden like a clean, white, empty
page once more.

And the snowdog stood at the
bottom of Big Hill wearing Tiger's
silly, woolly clothes...

For almost three…   whole…

weeks.